AN UNOFFICIAL GUIDE

THE

FORTNITE

GUIDE TO STAYING ALIVE

P9-BAV-510

TIPS AND
TRICKS FOR
EVERY KIND
OF PLAYER

DAMIEN KUHN

This edition © 2018 by Andrews McMeel Publishing

All rights reserved. Printed in the United States of America.
No part of this book may be used or reproduced in any
manner whatsoever without written permission except
in the case of reprints in the context of reviews.

Published in French under the title *Fortnite* Le Guide de Jeu
© 2018 404 éditions, a division of Édi8
12, avenue d'Italie, 75013 Paris, France

Fortnite is a registered trademark of Epic Games. All rights reserved.

This book is not an official *Fortnite* product. It is not
approved by or related to Epic Games.

Andrews McMeel Publishing
a division of Andrews McMeel Universal
1130 Walnut Street, Kansas City, Missouri 64106

www.andrewsmcmeel.com

18 19 20 21 22 RR2 10 9 8 7 6 5 4 3 2 1

ISBN: 978-1-4494-9939-6

Library of Congress Control Number: 2018954400

Made by:
LSC Communications US, LLC
Address and location of manufacturer:
1009 Sloan Street
Crawfordsville, IN 47933
1st Printing—9/21/18

ATTENTION: SCHOOLS AND BUSINESSES
Andrews McMeel books are available at quantity discounts with
bulk purchase for educational, business, or sales promotional use.
For information, please e-mail the Andrews McMeel Publishing
Special Sales Department: specialsales@amuniversal.com.

1. BEFORE YOU BEGIN

Published and developed by Epic Games, *Fortnite* has been a worldwide success since it was released in 2017, thanks to its Battle Royale game mode.

Available free of charge for download on PC, Mac, consoles (PS4, Xbox One, Nintendo Switch), Android, and iOS, *Fortnite Battle Royale* isn't an action or shooting game like the others: it's primarily a game of survival in which you'll need to be able to travel through hostile territory . . .

At first, everything seems fine: up to 100 players are on board a flying blue bus that's gliding smoothly over an ocean and gradually approaching an island.

Once the bus is above land, the driver opens the doors.

Are you hesitating to jump? Are you nervous about leaping into the void? Unfortunately, you have no choice: you have 30 seconds or less because you've just bought your ticket for the Battle Royale!

In the course of this wild adventure, you'll be moving through a fun, brightly colored world, where foothills and plains sit alongside cities and lakes. But you're not there to be a tourist!

There's only one law here: survival of the fittest. The other 99 players aren't there to just hang out—they're there to eliminate you. And it's a no-holds-barred battle. The island and its combatants take no pity. You need to always be on the lookout.

Every player dreams of one thing: being the last survivor and becoming Victory Royale. To do that, it's essential to have a few tricks on hand, and we'll be giving you those in this guide. That way, you'll be able to handle any situation, even the most unexpected.

GAME MODES

Whether you're on your own or playing with others, you're sure to find the game mode that suits you best.

NEW MODE AVAILABLE!

⚡ SOLO

PLAY

Solo mode is obviously when you're playing alone. You don't have any allies—it's just you and 99 other combatants. Only one fighter will remain. This is the most popular game mode.

If you're a beginner, it's the ideal mode for getting some practice against real players. Some of them are very experienced and will keep you on your toes. If you like a challenge and you want to make rapid progress, don't hesitate—just jump into solo mode. Take some risks, dare to go out in search of your enemies, and challenge them. Try out the weapons that are available to you and see what you think of them. Practice until you're familiar with them and you've mastered them. Some will undoubtedly be more familiar to you than others.

For **duo mode**, we recommend that you share the experience with a friend, but it's entirely possible to play with someone you don't know.

Here, 100 players are divided into teams of two people. Same map, same weapons available, and always the same objective: survival.

However, duo mode is different from solo mode, because it allows you to communicate. Communication will be essential and decisive. You might need a headset and mic or some other way to communicate with your comrade in arms. Warn your partner when you spy enemies. Create strategies and watch out for each other. Trade weapons, help each other out. The two of you can build structures as a team to be more efficient. Together, you'll be stronger.

If your teammate is unlucky enough to be hit by a rival and his health is drained, remember that he still has a second chance. You'll have a few seconds to revive him. However, if you're not fast enough and his executioner delivers another burst of gunfire, you'll find yourself alone.

Your companion will still be connected to the match but won't be able to play with you any longer. But he'll still be able to chat with you and see you. If he wants, he can start another game on his own or in mutiplayer mode.

Lastly, you can form a group and play in **squad mode**. Squad mode is definitely the most fun, and you won't be able to stop laughing.

If you're a beginner start with solo mode, then advance into squad mode. Get accustomed to the game commands and test your skills against your enemies. It's ideal for practicing one-on-one. Roam around the island to become more familiar with it. That way, you won't be in unknown territory when you have partners. When you feel ready, go for it!

If you have the chance to play alongside some experienced friends, their knowledge is good to draw on. They can offer advice and guide you throughout the match.

On the other hand, if you're a hardened player, be fearless and make the most of your experience in squad mode!

You can play single and duo squads using the fill button. Or, the 100 combatants can be divided into teams of three or four players. Here, communication is more critical than ever, and acting on your own is not recommended. Be generous: if you have a maximum supply of weapons, but one of your teammates is low, donate some. If you don't want to share anything, go back to solo mode! A squad means cooperation!

Be organized. Assign yourselves roles. One player can have the job of providing cover to one of your sidekicks with sniper fire; someone else can be responsible for demolishing enemy structures; the two others can attack enemies who get close. Always stay grouped together. Don't venture out alone like some knight in shining armor. Your rivals will take on the task of bringing you back down to earth.

As with the previous mode, it's possible to take care of your friend, as long as you arrive in time. That's why you shouldn't go it alone—your teammates will suffer the consequences. Nonetheless, so long as one player on the team is alive, the match continues. Avenge your lost friends and bring that blasted Victory Royale down a notch!

If your friends aren't available for a little jaunt out to the island, play with people you don't know. The drawback is that you don't know their playing level in advance. Some may be beginners who will slow you down. But keep playing as a team anyway.

Sometimes you'll come across people who don't take it seriously, and that can be frustrating.

On the other hand, you may meet up with experienced players. Observe how they play, follow their example, ask them for advice—there's a lot you can learn from your teammates.

Fortnite Battle Royale offers what are called "limited time" game modes on a regular basis. Those modes keep the game interesting and let you vary your style of play. Here are a few of them:

50 v 50 mode is completely different from the modes we described earlier. You are in an army of 50 soldiers against another army with the same number of soldiers. Shots are fired in every direction, and structures appear on all sides. Your sidekicks are laid low by bullets, but so are your enemies.

But where do you start? Defend your colors to the end and revive your brothers who have fallen in combat. The army that wipes out all of the enemy soldiers is the victor.

🔸 **Solid Gold mode** lets you fight only with legendary weapons. If you're unlucky in your traditional matches and you only have small-caliber rounds, you can recover with this mode. What fun it is to find top-of-the-line artillery in every chest and every house!

🔸 Have you had an especially bad day? The **High Explosives mode** is sure to help you let off some steam. Unwind by blowing up everything in your path using grenades and rocket launchers! Nothing is available except for explosive weapons. Like Solid Gold mode, High Explosives mode is ideal for handling weapons that you rarely come across in the traditional games.

🔸 Had enough of endless matches? Try **Blitz mode**! There's a fast-approaching storm. It's impossible to hide and camp for very long. Players have no time to lose in finding weapons, with only the resources at hand. The zone shrinks quickly, so you have to fight. Blitz is a perfect mode for practicing quick decision-making. You don't have time to camp. It forces you to build and attack your enemies. It's ideal for developing your reflexes.

🔸 Good news! The **Playground LTM mode** lets you practice the way you like with your friends. Kill one another, build structures, and practice shooting without being bothered by other players.

THE BATTLE PASS

*F*ortnite *Battle Royale* operates by seasons.

With each new season, a new battle pass is available for purchase. You can buy it in the in-game store for the price of 950 V-Bucks.

That pass gives you access to 100 items. That means skins, V-Bucks, pickaxes, dances, and various accessories for customizing your character could be yours. It gives you two additional daily challenges, as well as special weekly challenges.

However if you don't want to buy the battle pass, you can win items by earning free battle pass tiers.

To do this, perform the daily and weekly challenges for the battle pass. For each challenge you successfully complete, you win battle stars. Once you have 10 stars, you get a new tier and you win an item.

Each time you play and kill your enemies, your rank increases, you gain XP (experience points), and level up. Leveling up is another way of winning battle stars. A few free items can also be won.

Once one season ends and another begins, everyone starts all over again at zero.

But don't panic—you keep all the items you've won!

Fitting out your character with a costume or some other item won't make you stronger than everyone else. But you'll eliminate your enemies with class, and that's pretty cool!

Remember! *Fortnite* is updated on a regular basis with each new season. The challenges, the accessories, and even the map may change with every new update.

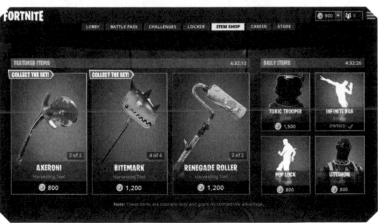

2. THE MAP

 THE ENVIRONMENT

The Battle Royale takes place on an island, where you'll find different types of landscapes.

From the city to the countryside to the mountain, there's something for every taste.

The main city is Tilted Towers. It's located in the center of the island and consists of numerous buildings, including a clock tower. Some buildings have as many as four stories: be sure not to stumble if you find yourself on the roof!

The city is dangerous and very crowded; the players who land there are generally the most experienced. In the city, being Victory Royale is not their priority; they're interested in beating their kill record.

The map also includes other cities, like Pleasant Park, Greasy Grove, and Retail Row. Consisting primarily of houses with yards, these towns are much less imposing than Tilted Towers but ideal for starting a match on the right foot. We'll explain why in the next section . . .

Finally, in the farthest corners of the map, you can visit small villages with no more than two or three houses.

The island also has areas of nature, such as wide-open plains, with scattered trees as far as you can see. Venturing there is dangerous, because you're out in the open and thus much more vulnerable to attack. But these expansive areas take up a large portion of the map, so you'll be forced to travel through them in order to get from one city to another. Plus, that's where you can collect resources, such as wood, for the structures you build. We'll address that topic in detail later on.

To limit the damage you might sustain on the plains, you can climb the foothills and mountains, where you can hide and get an unobstructed view of the surroundings and your enemies. Be careful descending: take an existing path or build stairs. Do you love wild sensations? You can also slide along the walls to get down. However, be careful when landing—it would be foolish to lose health by falling.

How can you resist a quick swim? Apart from the ocean surrounding the island, take a dip in Loot Lake! Of course, you can't be sure you won't be seen and water does make you slower.

After a meteorite fell, a number of craters appeared in Season 4. The Dusty Divot area was heavily affected, and an enormous crater covered a wide area.

In its wake, the meteorite left a little gift for players: anti-gravity hop rocks. You could find them around and inside craters. They were a beautiful blue color and when you ate a hop rock, it let you jump farther and stay in the air longer. It was ideal for dominating your enemy. But the effects only lasted for about 30 seconds. In Season 5 the craters were removed and this area is abandoned and overgrown with grassland, trees, and small ponds.

Other new locations have made an appearance since the start of Season 4:

🔸 On the eastern side of the island, south of Lonely Lodge, a mansion overlooks the ocean. This mansion has countless rooms, as well as a strange basement that's been transformed into a laboratory.

🔸 Next to Snobby Shores, a mountain houses a secret base as well as a rocket. The rocket launched at the end of Season 4.

🔸 On the northeast end of the map, you'll find Risky Reels. You can visit its outdoor theater as well as a crater and its famous rocks.

🔸 Feeling festive? Head to the warehouses in the south to dance in a club!

🔋 You can also take a look at Paradise Palms, which is located in the new desert ecosystem: it's an abandoned spot, but with a racetrack and dinosaur statues. Otherwise, you can visit Lazy Links in the north, where you'll find a gigantic villa with a tennis court, golf course, and swimming pool.

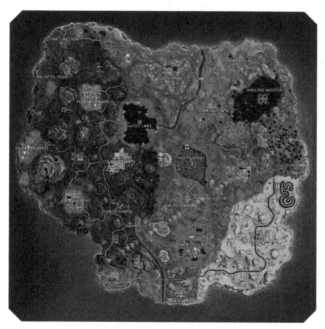

THE STORM

Weather conditions on the island can be a little unpredictable. A terrible storm is constantly raging, so monitor your map at all times to be sure you don't get trapped. Whenever you're a prisoner of the storm, your health drops: the first storm costs you 1 health point (HP) per second; the second, 2 HPs per second; the third, 5 HPs per second; and so on. They become increasingly violent and destructive as you go along.

An alarm goes off to signal that the storm is beginning.

On your map, a white circle appears. That's the area you need to reach in order to be safe.

The storm happens in waves. For several minutes, it's inactive, so you aren't risking anything. But after awhile, it starts up again. Then the players are forced to head back to the area indicated by the white circle.

A timer located in the upper-right corner of your screen tells you the amount of time left until the next storm; when the storm is raging, the timer indicates how long you need to remain sheltered.

As soon as the storm reaches the white circle, a new, smaller circle appears in the distance.

As the end of the match approaches, the circle grows smaller. So the likelihood of encountering survivors grows dangerously higher. You won't be able to hide forever—you'll have to return to combat.

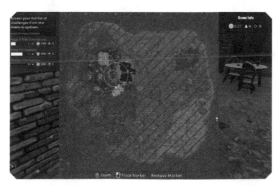

There are several tricks for managing this freak weather phenomenon:

💧 First, always keep an eye on your map and think ahead.

💧 If you're on the western side of the island and the storm area appears at the western tip, start moving immediately. Don't wait until the last minute to leave!

💧 If the storm area suddenly appears fairly close, don't panic! You still have an adequate amount of time left. Continue to search the area or fight off enemies. You'll even be allowed within the white circle after the storm has started. But don't wait until it's a few meters away—plan ahead!

💧 If you're naturally lucky, you may already be in the white circle. Then you have nothing to worry about. Nonetheless, look over your map to find the next secure location.

💧 If the storm is coming dangerously close, there's only one solution: run to the white circle to seek cover! Look at your map and follow the white line. That's the shortest route.

Go straight in that direction; don't zigzag. If by some misfortune there's an obstacle in the way, such as a hill, build stairs to get over it. You'll lose less time than by going around it.

If you see enemies in the same area as you, don't pay any attention to them and don't engage in combat. However, if an enemy is in front of you and you can bring him down from behind while you're on your way, go for it!

 If you find yourself inside the storm, but you have enough bandages, chug jugs, and/or medkits in your inventory, that may save you. Once you're a prisoner, your health drains away little by little. When your health approaches 30, stop and take care of yourself. Once your health is higher, get moving again. Repeat as often as necessary until you've escaped the miserable storm.

And if you don't have enough healing items with you, run—and say your prayers!

3. GETTING OFF TO A GOOD START

When a match begins, you're in the company of 99 or fewer other players, having to wait on Spawn Island, which is in a kind of field that looks more like a crazy playground. Some people are dancing, others are running in every direction. Some stand still, waiting for the game to begin.

A few weapons are scattered around. Grab them at once so you can train yourself how to shoot. During this time, you can't be injured and you can't kill anyone. So train yourself to shoot and kill anything that moves—even those aspiring dancers. You don't get to keep these weapons once the game starts.

You should also take the opportunity to cut some wood, collect some stones and metal, and build structures.

After you've waited awhile, it's time to board the flying bus. One good thing is that the bus drivers never go on vacation.

CHOOSING YOUR DESTINATION

During the time just before boarding, you can look over the map and the route that the bus plans to take. There's no point in negotiating with drivers—or slipping a bill into their pocket—so that they'll drop you where you want to go. They're not your private driver!

Whether you're playing alone, in duo mode, or squad mode, choosing a destination is critical. Let's say you're playing as part of a squad. If you go off in opposite directions, your chances of survival are tiny. Always come to an agreement on your arrival location.

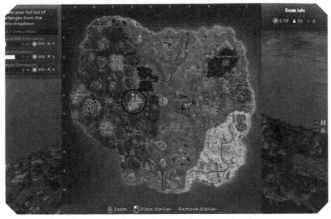

The player has placed her marker on Tilted Towers.

We recommend that you parachute in differently depending on the type of player you are.

If your primary goal is to kill as many enemies as possible, you can opt for several tactics:

🔥 As soon as the bus doors open, jump and head for the nearest city. A fair number of players will follow you. Be ready to do battle.

🔥 You can also wait a little and go to Tilted Towers, which has the reputation of being a real battleground.

On the other hand, if your goal is to not have a high kill count but to survive and reach Victory Royale, we advise you to play it safe.

Choose a spot that's less frequented. Head for open countryside, or a city like Pleasant Park or Retail Row. Then there will be fewer of you and you'll be less exposed to danger. Offering plenty of weapons and resources for building, those smaller towns are ideal for starting a match right.

If you want to avoid danger at all costs and eliminate the likelihood of encountering enemies, go to the far end of the map, near the coasts. There is very little chance that other players will be nearby. However, you're taking a big risk: it's possible that you'll be in the area threatened by the storm right away. So you'll have less time to scope out the area and collect resources.

THE PROPER WAY TO JUMP

You have to do more than just choose your destination . . . You also need to know how to get there before anyone else, so you need to jump the right way.

After you've marked your arrival location on the map, prepare to go all out.

It's important never to jump right on top of the city or place you want. That's a mistake a lot of players make. When you jump like that, you're forced to wait until you're on top of your destination. Meanwhile, the players who jumped well ahead of you will already be gliding calmly toward the city while you're still in the sky.

So you should constantly evaluate the distance, then jump at the right moment.

Remember: Your parachute opens automatically at a certain altitude. In order to delay opening the parachute for as long as possible, don't fly too closely over a hill (unless it's your destination), because your glider will activate too soon.

Always aim for the lowest point. The later your parachute opens, the better your chances of arriving at your goal before the others.

The player has thought ahead and will probably be the first to arrive at Tilted Towers.

MANAGING THE FIRST MINUTES OF THE MATCH

Don't forget that the goal of *Fortnite Battle Royale* is survival. At the start of the game, we advise you not to jump near the line where the bus passes, because that's the option that most players—your potential murderers—will choose. Parachute into a more remote spot.

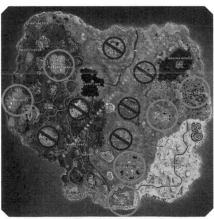

When you're approaching your destination, we recommend that you always land on the roof of a building. Whenever possible, choose a house where no one has landed, and avoid the city center. If you're playing as a duo, land on houses that are close together, so you can help each other.

If you're fighting as a squad, you shouldn't all land on the same residence, because there won't be enough weapons for all four of you. But try to land on neighboring houses: in the event of an attack you'll be able to support each other more quickly.

Once you've landed, run across the entire roof. If you hear a funny noise, that means you're on top of a chest. The noise gets louder as you get closer to the chest. It contains weapons and resources. Make a hole in the roof with your pickaxe and gather the loot.

Some houses may not have a lot of loot to offer. In that case, you'll have to choose from among several options:

🔥 The first is to head directly for an enemy and engage in combat. Go to the house where the enemy is located, preferably landing on the roof. Once you're inside, move in a crouch so you don't make noise, and exterminate the enemy as soon as you have the opportunity.

Once the player has been killed, take his or her batch of weapons and resources. That's an effective but risky solution. We recommend it to experienced players.

🍗 Another option is to stay armed and hidden inside a house. Very few players only search one building. It's very likely that you'll have a visitor. Always remember to close the doors behind you. A house with open doors is one that's been searched or is occupied. With the doors closed, you won't give any indication that you're present. Moreover, you'll hear any enemies when they open the doors. Increase the volume so as to hear the enemy's movements. Carefully hide yourself in an upstairs room, and take him by surprise when he opens the door.

🍗 The third strategy is to go to another house. There's a slight chance that no one will have gone there yet. It's also possible that someone has already visited the house and left some weapons behind.

🍗 One final and more drastic step is to change cities, although you run the risk of running into enemies along the way.

Starting the game with a lot of resources is essential for survival.

So remember to collect wood, stone, and metal. Destroy the furniture in your house and tap the walls or even the floor. Caution: don't demolish the structure of a house completely, or you'll be visible from outside. Also, pay attention to the noise made by your blows: you could attract the attention of your enemies.

Continue collecting items when you're moving around outside.

Don't forget to check your map so you're not surprised by the storm. Think ahead and head for the safe zone indicated by the white circle, if you're not there already.

When you're moving around outdoors, jump while you run. If a well-hidden sniper wants to eliminate you, you'll make it significantly more difficult.

Whatever happens, you'll be able to return fire using the weapons you carefully obtained from the chests.

4. GATHERING SUPPLIES

Starting a game with loot is good, but starting with a rocket launcher is even better!

In order to survive the Battle Royale, it's essential to be properly equipped. You'll find weapons on the ground and in buildings. But those aren't the only places.

CHESTS

The most important way to get the proper equipment is to locate chests. Those chests give off a sound: the louder the signal, the closer you are.

Chests are distributed all over the map. You're much more likely to find one in the big cities. But don't worry—they're also in the countryside and even the most unlikely places, such as a cave, a mine, a doghouse, the trailer of a truck, or even a boat in the middle of a lake. Some can even be found at the top of a hill or a tower.

In houses, chests are generally difficult to access, since they may be hidden under roofs or in the basement. In some cases you'll have to explore the whole house from top to bottom before finding one.

Note that a chest always appears in the same place, but not necessarily in every match. Whenever possible, try to remember where the chest was located. That will be extremely helpful to you, especially at the start of the match. In fact, once you've jumped from the bus, plan to land at a spot where you know the location of the chest. That will give you an advantage.

Once you've discovered the chest, all you have to do is open it and use what's inside.

Be careful not to destroy it by pounding on it or damaging the ground it sits on.

A chest contains several accessories that will help you throughout the match. You'll always find a weapon with ammo; you may also find building resources (20 pieces of wood, stone, or metal), some shield potions, and healing.

⫷━ LLAMAS ━⫸

L ooking for a llama is like looking for a needle in a haystack.

They're extremely rare—you'll only find three per match. Their locations vary each time, so it's impossible to predict where they will appear.

If you do see one, we recommend that you take advantage of it. However, don't rush up to it; look around first. You may not be the only one who's spotted it! Once you've plotted an escape route, approach this odd little piñata cautiously. Build four walls around it so as to protect yourself against shots or prying eyes. Add a roof as a precaution, especially near a hill.

Wait about five seconds before unlocking the llama, then remove its contents. Or you can save time by destroying it with a weapon. Be careful not to do that with a chest, though, because the items inside will also be destroyed.

Once the llama is open, you can take the resources: 200 of each material—wood, stone, and metal—which you can use to get yourself out of all kinds of trouble. The llama was even more generous in the past, offering 500 of each item. Let's hope those days return soon . . .

You can also fill up on ammo, traps, potions, and healing. The llama offers much more than the chests.

Its only faults are that it doesn't have weapons or ammo for explosive weapons.

SUPPLY DROPS

Supply drops fall from the sky on a regular basis. Blue smoke indicates the spot on the ground where a supply drop landed. You will undoubtedly not be the only one to see it. That's why we advise you to be extremely cautious. A supply drop can definitely contain a gold mine: you may find a legendary weapon, ammo, traps, shields, and healing. But if you're already well equipped, it may not be essential to worry about it.

Be careful not to endanger yourself by rushing directly at it. As with the llamas, scan the area and verify that the coast is clear. There's a strong chance that enemies are trying to seize it as well.

If you're impatient, you can shoot at the balloon to make the crate drop faster. But the balloon is quite resistant, so make sure you have enough ammunition. And remember that by shooting, you'll tell the other players where you are.

Another solution is to build stairs and then a platform at a height so that the balloon will land faster. That's a risky operation, because you'll be visible from fairly far away.

If you want to be more careful, remain at a distance and quietly wait for the supply drop to land. Once the precious cargo is on the ground, build four walls around it and help yourself. Then leave the area quickly.

If you're looking for kills, hide yourself and eliminate the players who unwisely make a charge for it; supply drops serve as perfect bait.

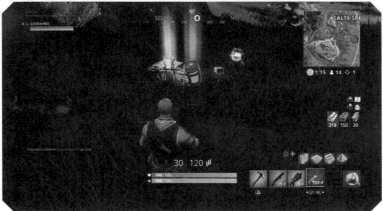

VENDING MACHINES

Vending machines are scattered across various locations on the island. Players can use them to obtain a weapon using their resources (wood, stone, or metal). We recommend that you use a vending machine if your inventory is low or the machine has your favorite weapon.

And don't forget to check whether you have enough resources before buying—the vending machines are especially greedy.

THE AMMO BOX

These little green boxes should not be overlooked. They're most often found in buildings under roofs or stairs or on shelves. They provide the necessary ammunition to ensure you don't run out.

5. THE FIGHTER'S EQUIPMENT

 **WEAPONS**

If you don't have weapons, you'll never get the Victory Royale! It goes without saying that without weapons, you won't make it very far.

Fortnite offers an extensive artillery with which to adapt to and tackle any situation.

Each weapon is associated with a color: gray weapons are common, while green weapons are a little less so. Blue weapons are rare, and purple weapons are described as epic. The best are gold weapons, which are obviously the most difficult to find. A single weapon can have several different rarities.

Suppose you have a gray assault rifle. If by chance you come across another assault rifle in blue (meaning it's rare), trade yours for that one.

The rarer your weapon, the larger the damage. Its accuracy and the damage it can inflict are enhanced. The reload times are faster as well, which is no small thing.

Gray	Green	Blue	Purple	Gold
Common	Uncommon	Rare	Epic	Legendary

PISTOLS

PISTOL

RARITY: COMMON, UNCOMMON, RARE

This is a widely used weapon that you can easily find throughout the game. However, we recommend that you only use it at the

start of the game or if you have nothing else available. When used at close range, you'll have a chance to get away, thanks to its rate of fire.

REVOLVER

RARITY: COMMON, UNCOMMON, RARE

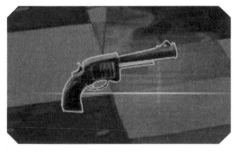

You know the face you make when you're served spinach? That's a little like the look on your face when you get a revolver.

With their very slow rate of fire, revolvers won't get you out of a tough spot. But for the most hardened combatants who can see their enemy's head perfectly, a revolver can prove very effective.

HAND CANNON

RARITY: EPIC, LEGENDARY

This weapon causes heavy damage to your opponent. But because of its slow fire rate, we recommend it only for the most experienced players who can target the head with no difficulty.

SUPPRESSED PISTOL

RARITY: EPIC, LEGENDARY

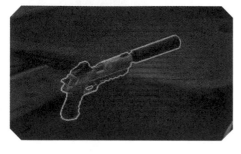

This is the best pistol you can find. It's quiet, easy to handle, and effective, and it allows you to inflict heavy damage. It can be used at medium range (unlike the revolver) and reloaded quickly.

DUAL PISTOLS

RARITY: EPIC, LEGENDARY

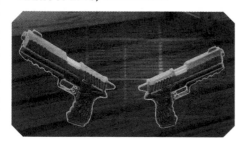

The dual pistol—the legendary weapon from *Tomb Raider*—is effective. Thanks to its good firing speed, you can win duels at short distances.

SMGS

SUBMACHINE GUN

RARITY: COMMON, UNCOMMON, RARE

This weapon has an impressive fire rate.

It's very effective at short distances, so we recommend it to players who have difficulty with the shotgun.

SUPPRESSED SUBMACHINE GUN

RARITY: COMMON, UNCOMMON, RARE

Unlike the previous weapon, this gun fires fewer bullets per second, but inflicts more damage. Thanks to its silencer, it is also quiet.

DRUM GUN

RARITY: UNCOMMON, RARE

Because of its excellent rate of fire and the respectable amount of damage it can cause, the drum gun is a good compromise between a simple SMG and an assault rifle. It will be most suitable for medium-range distances.

SHOTGUNS

PUMP SHOTGUN

RARITY: UNCOMMON, RARE

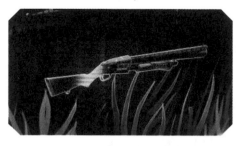

Extremely effective in close-range combat, this weapon can be used to inflict heavy damage. Its only downside is its slow fire rate. Be sure your shooting is accurate!

TACTICAL SHOTGUN

RARITY: COMMON, UNCOMMON, RARE

This weapon is a classic! It's easy to handle, even for the inexperienced, and offers an impressive fire rate. It certainly doesn't inflict as much damage as the pump shotgun, but your chances of hitting your enemy are much higher.

HEAVY SHOTGUN

RARITY: EPIC, LEGENDARY

This weapon inflicts less damage than a standard shotgun. On the other hand, its perfectly good fire rate and added accuracy will be useful in medium-range fighting.

ASSAULT RIFLES

ASSAULT RIFLE

RARITY: COMMON, UNCOMMON, RARE, EPIC, LEGENDARY

A must-have! Really, its accuracy, its effectiveness at every distance, its good fire rate, and the damage it inflicts make it an essential weapon.

BURST ASSAULT RIFLE

RARITY: COMMON, UNCOMMON, RARE, EPIC, LEGENDARY

A burst assault rifle has a fairly slow or even extremely slow fire rate. Each burst delivers three bullets. We recommend that you use it for medium or long distances. If you're face-to-face with an enemy, a burst rifle would quickly become a handicap.

FAMAS

RARITY: EPIC, LEGENDARY

The FAMAS bears a close resemblance to the burst assault rifle. But its increased power tends to set it apart.

SCOPED ASSAULT RIFLE

RARITY: RARE, EPIC

Thanks to its scope, this assault rifle offers laser precision. Unlike the previous rifles, this one has no dispersion, which

means the bullet travels straight to its target. Very useful for medium and long-range shooting, this weapon is an excellent sniper rifle.

THERMAL SCOPED ASSAULT RIFLE

RARITY: EPIC, LEGENDARY

This weapon is much more powerful than the scoped assault

rifle. Moreover, the thermal scope gives you a considerable advantage over your enemies. You'll be able to spy other players, chests, and supplies from a distance.

SCAR (SUPRESSED COMBAT ASSAULT RIFLE)

RARITY: EPIC, LEGENDARY

This assault rifle is a little like the Cristiano Ronaldo of soccer or the Drake of the music world. It's beautiful, elegant, and as rare as water in the desert. Its powerful impact, fire rate, and precision make it THE versatile rifle to have on hand. It can be used to eliminate your worst enemies and destroy the sturdiest structures. We often say "nothing is perfect," but the SCAR tends to prove the opposite. Trying is believing!

SNIPER RIFLES

HUNTING RIFLE

RARITY: UNCOMMON, RARE

Don't underestimate this! Though it lacks a scope, this rifle is still a good weapon. Even at long distances, two bullets will be enough to reduce your enemy to a pile of ash.

BOLT-ACTION SNIPER RIFLE

RARITY: RARE, EPIC, LEGENDARY

An enemy without a shield can be taken down in one shot with this scoped rifle. It's the most powerful of the sniper rifles. On the other hand, its extremely long reloading time is a real handicap. Be patient—it's better to hit your mark on the first try.

SEMI-AUTO SNIPER RIFLE

RARITY: EPIC, LEGENDARY

Thanks to its scope, this sniper rifle is more accurate than the hunting rifle, and two bullets will be enough to knock out any enemy (without a shield). Its excellent fire rate makes this a tremendously powerful weapon.

HEAVY WEAPONS

MINIGUN

RARITY: EPIC, LEGENDARY

When you run into one of these for the first time, you may think of yourself as a warrior, but you'll become bored with

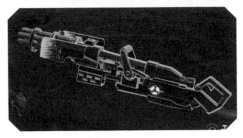

it soon enough. First of all, it takes a long time to start up: you'll think you're at the wheel of an old car! And its lack of precision poses an obstacle. On the positive side, the minigun is an effective tool for destroying enemy structures.

LIGHT MACHINE GUN

RARITY: RARE, EPIC

This weapon is fairly difficult to find. Thanks to its excellent fire rate, it's effective in every situation, at both near and far range. The icing on the cake is the aggressive noise it puts out.

GRENADE LAUNCHER

RARITY: RARE, EPIC, LEGENDARY

The grenade launcher is very useful for destroying enemy structures. However, its maneuverability does not make it the most accurate heavy weapon, and you'll undoubtedly need several grenades to come close to your rival.

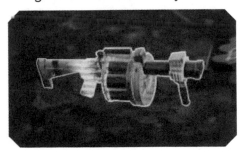

ROCKET LAUNCHER

RARITY: RARE, EPIC, LEGENDARY

Ideal for demolishing construction, this weapon can also prove a lifesaver in one-on-one combat. Very few opponents can withstand a rocket. However, be careful not to shoot at an enemy who's too close—you may be hurt as well! Needless to say, this is not one of the quietest weapons. A piercing noise follows the shot, giving valuable information about your location.

PICKAXE

This is the massively destructive weapon to have on hand at all costs. A single blow will be enough to wipe out your enemies and make it to the top . . . No, no, we're joking! The pickaxe is used to help gather resources. But blows from a pickaxe can certainly inflict some damage—albeit minimal damage—on an enemy.

EXPLOSIVES

They can save the day on numerous occasions. Don't overlook them!

GRENADE

RARITY: COMMON

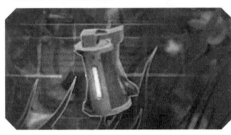

These explosives are easy to find and extremely useful. You can use them to destroy structures but also to defend yourself. Let's take an example: you're on the second floor of a house, but the ground floor is occupied by an assailant. Throw the grenades down the stairs. With a little luck, your enemy will be hit and sustain serious injuries.

BOOGIE BOMB

RARITY: RARE

Any enemies hit by the explosion of the Boogie Bomb will start dancing for five seconds. Make the most of it and eliminate them in time to the music! Just be careful not to throw it too close to yourself, unless you're in the mood to sway your hips.

CLINGER

RARITY: UNCOMMON

If you manage to throw this on opponents, they will be unable to get rid of it. Unless they have a shield, it's certain death.

REMOTE EXPLOSIVES

RARITY: RARE

Place these explosives carefully in a house or structure, stand back, and watch everything explode. Guaranteed carnage!

IMPULSE GRENADE

RARITY: RARE

This is a very good weapon if you find yourself targeted by one or more enemies: throw this grenade in their midst and immediately your enemies will be thrown backwards. You can also use it when enemies are up high: the grenade will propel them backward and cause them to fall.

STINK BOMB

RARITY: EPIC

This bomb gives off a large toxic cloud. For nine seconds, anyone who breathes the gas loses 5 health every half-second. It's a perfect weapon for dislodging players from their hiding places. Be careful not to throw it too close to your allies.

HEALING AND PROTECTION

There are very few battles from which you'll emerge totally unscathed. Fortunately, *Fortnite* provides various items that you can use to treat and protect yourself. They're generally available in chests and supply drops and on the ground.

In order to use a healing item, you have to stay in place. You can't yet treat yourself while walking or running. Stay vigilant and, whenever possible, hide yourself so you can recover in peace.

BANDAGES

RARITY: COMMON

This healing item takes five seconds to give you back 15 health. However, these bandages won't work if your character has 75 or more health.

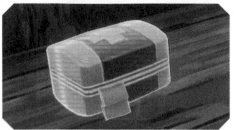

MEDKIT

RARITY: UNCOMMON

Unlike the bandages, a medkit restores all of your health. You'll need to wait 10 seconds.

SMALL SHIELD POTION

RARITY: UNCOMMON

This small potion is easy to find and grants 25 shield in just two

seconds. The shield offers you a second chance, because it protects your health. Unfortunately the potion can't be used if your shield is at 50 or more.

SHIELD POTION

RARITY: RARE

This large potion gives you 50 shield in five seconds, which makes it one of the best healing items.

SLURP JUICE

RARITY: EPIC

This concoction can be swallowed down in three seconds.

Unlike the other potions, you need

to wait 25 seconds in order for your gauge to rise 75 shield.
Its primary advantage is that it can be used up to 75 health.

CHUG JUG

RARITY: LEGENDARY

After you drink this delicious potion, wait 15 seconds. That's long, but worth it: it restores you to maximum health and shield. More than just an energy drink, that's for sure, but it's very rare. Naturally . . .

APPLES

RARITY: UNCOMMON

Eat five fruits and vegetables every day! An apple gives you five health, which is quite handy when you have no medkits available. Unfortunately, you can't store this fruit in your inventory. You need to eat it at the foot of the apple tree.

MUSHROOMS

RARITY: UNCOMMON

Devouring a mushroom gives you 5 shield. Don't consume in moderation! Like the apples, you can't keep them with you.

ACCESSORIES

*F*ortnite Battle Royale puts various accessories at your disposal. Use them alongside your weapons to increase your chances of survival.

DAMAGE TRAP

RARITY: UNCOMMON

The trap can be placed on the ground or on any surface that accepts traps. So be cunning: place it so your enemies won't see it. If they pass nearby, it's activated automatically (except on you). Show some imagination!

In a house, for example, you can place it on the ceiling above a stairway. If your enemy is on the ground floor and decides to go upstairs, it's quite likely he or she will be trapped by passing underneath it.

BUSH

RARITY: LEGENDARY

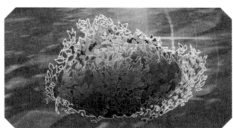

When properly used, the bush is a useful tool. You should turn to it first when you're moving across the plains, so as to mislead your enemy. In a building, on the other hand, you'll be quickly identified, and one bullet is enough to deactivate it.

LAUNCH PAD

RARITY: EPIC

Too lazy to walk? Want an easy way out? Set up your launch pad, jump, and you're all set! Your glider will deploy so you can change location.

BOUNCER TRAP

RARITY: RARE

The bouncer trap will bounce anyone into the air several meters. You can also use it yourself to reach the top of a structure. With this accessory, you won't be injured by a fall, so take advantage of that and use it to, say, descend quickly from a mountain peak: normally you would lose your life, but by relying on the bouncer trap you'll be unharmed. Convenient!

COZY CAMPFIRE

RARITY: RARE

Get out the hot dogs and marshmallows!

Once it's set up, the campfire will replenish your energy at 2 health per second. It's a real asset, especially when you're playing as part of a duo or squad, since everyone benefits.

PORT-A-FORT

RARITY: EPIC

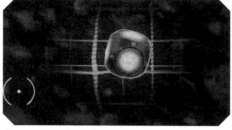

If you have few resources and you're being attacked from outside, activate your fort! A metal tower automatically rises up from the ground, allowing you to get the upper hand on your enemy. Unfortunately, it's not a very durable structure. So it makes more sense to find the resources for building a more robust shelter.

SHOPPING CART

RARITY: COMMON

These are found primarily in the cities. You can use the shopping cart to move around more quickly, either alone or with a friend. It's better to use these in solo or duo mode. In a squad, you'll end up abandoning the rest of your team, unless you have two of them.

The passenger can use weapons while the driver steers, making this an interesting accessory. Plus, the cart can get you out of some very tricky situations. If you're trapped by the storm, hold on tight and make a rush for the safe zone! Or steer it through a rift to teleport to a nearby safe space.

ATK (ALL TERRAIN KART)

RARITY: COMMON

A step up from the shopping cart added in Season 5, this can be used to cruise or as an attack vehicle with up to four teammates. The roof can be used as a bounce pad.

THE STANDARD EQUIPMENT TO HAVE ON HAND

Every player has his or her own playing methods and preferences. You don't always find the weapons you want, and you sometimes have to rely on luck to get the best caliber weapons. So here we offer an example of the ideal equipment:

🔹 an assault rifle that's effective in every situation: a scoped assault rifle or a SCAR;

🔹 a shotgun for all close combat: a tactical shotgun;

🔹 a long-range rifle: a hunting or semi-automatic rifle;

🔹 a heavy weapon for demolishing structures, such as a rocket launcher;

🔹 healing: potions, bandages, or medkits.

When several of you are playing together, assign tasks among yourselves. You don't all have to keep the same inventory

For example, in squad mode, one player can be responsible for enemies in the distance. That player should be equipped with a long-range rifle and the sniper bullets you collect along the way.

Task another player with destroying enemy structures with the help of a heavy weapon, such as a rocket launcher and the appropriate ammunition.

6. RESOURCES

To survive the Battle Royale, it's not enough just to be well armed. You also need to know how to build attack and defensive structures. For that, you need to collect as many resources as possible. Of course, you'll find some materials in the chests or on the ground, but the best thing to do will be to gather them in nature. The pickaxe will be your best friend.

 WOOD

Wood is the easiest resource to obtain. Just swing at walls, floors, and ceilings in houses. Trees obviously provide a large quantity of wood as well. But when you're attacking a tree with your pickaxe, remember the environment. Don't destroy it completely. The tree will disappear and a few leaves will fall. If enemies are close by, you'll give them valuable information about your position.

Don't hesitate to strike at wood pallets: they're easily destroyed and offer quite a lot of resources.

Although it's perfect for building a structure quickly, wood is less resistant to bullets than any other material. So we advise you to not use it when fighting a duel. You can also draw on wood to provide shelter when you're using a healing item.

STONE

Stone is found primarily in the walls of stone houses. You can also find rocks in nature, so don't hesitate to collect them.

On the other hand, there's no point in striking at mountain rock: you won't be able to collect stone that way!

Unlike wood, building a stone structure takes more time. However, stone is more resistant. Choose stone when your enemies are well armed and can quickly destroy your wood structures: you'll be giving them a bigger headache to deal with.

 METAL

Metal is the least common resource. You can strike cars, trucks, and containers to obtain it. Make sure there are no enemies nearby, because collecting metal is not a very quiet activity. Some vehicles will sound an alarm, or the horn will go off.

Of the three materials, metal is the most resistant. But building a metal structure takes time, and you need to have patience.

Prioritize metal at the end of the game, when the combat area will have shrunk significantly. Duels generally end with rocket launchers, so it's better to have a metal structure than one made from wood.

7. CONSTRUCTION

Unless you build structures, it's nearly impossible to survive in *Fortnite Battle Royale*.

As we saw in the previous section, you have three building materials available: wood, stone, and metal, which you can obtain throughout the game and use to build floors, stairs, walls, pyramids, and even roofs.

Each of those materials has its advantages and disadvantages. For example, you can erect a wall made of wood in just five seconds, but it only has 200 health. Floors, stairs, and roofs have 190 health. So you can build most rapidly with wood, but unfortunately it's the easiest material to destroy.

A stone wall has 300 health, but takes about 12 seconds to build. It's actually an excellent alternative to a wood wall in terms of resistance. Nonetheless, 12 seconds is a long time: your enemies have plenty of time to disrupt your work. As for floors, stairs, and roofs, they each have 280 health.

If you build a metal wall, you'll need to wait virtually 20 seconds to gain the 400 health. Make sure you can't be seen until the health for your construction is full. Other metal structures have resistance of 370 health.

Bear that information in mind when deciding on what to build.

In order to build any structure, you must first select what you want at the bottom right of the screen.

Then place the structure wherever you like and confirm your choice. Depending on how you have oriented the structure and where you're located, it's possible that the structure won't work. In that case, adopt a different strategy. You may also find that you don't have enough resources.

Don't get yourself bogged down; train yourself to switch quickly between floors, stairs, walls, and roofs, because in a duel your reaction time will be critical. It would be foolish to panic and build a roof instead of a wall as your enemy is approaching.

STAIRWAYS

Stairs are exceptionally helpful, first and foremost because they provide a way to move around safely. If you want to get up on the roof of a house quickly, avoid going inside: not only do you risk encountering other players but the house may have a trap.

So we advise you to enter a house from the top whenever possible, using a stairway. Don't use stone or metal for that; wood will do fine.

The same holds true if, for example, you're trying to reach a chest in a basement. A wood stairway will do the trick.

When it comes to terrain, stairs are especially useful for scaling mountains and hills, especially since some are completely inaccessible on foot. In that case, always build a stairway beside a mountainside or hillside. If you don't build it by following the incline and an opponent decides to have some fun by pulling on its base, you'll fall. But with this technique, your enemies will find it much more difficult to pursue their evil ways.

Stairs can also be used to attack your opponents by gaining height. For that, we recommend you use the "double stair/wall" method, which consists of placing two stairways side by side, then building two walls to protect them. Individual stairways are easy to destroy, whereas this will pose much more of a challenge to your enemies.

 **FLOORS**

You'll primarily use floors inside your structures to get around and prevent a fall.

They will also be useful for moving around at a height. For example, if you need to get over an obstacle, construct stairs, then build a kind of bridge by using floors. Then build more stairs to get down again.

 WALLS

Walls are essential to survival and usually used for defense; they're your best friend during the entire Battle Royale. Think about it: have you ever seen a military base without walls? No? Neither have we.

But you don't always need to build a castle to defend yourself!

If the shots are coming from straight ahead, build a line of two walls in front of you, using stone or wood. Place two stairways behind them—you can use them as a ramp to help you locate where the shots are coming from more accurately and return fire. Pay attention to the impact from the bullets! Consider repairing your structure if it's losing too much health.

Here's another situation: let's say you're strolling through an open plain and suddenly shots come at you from all sides. Immediately build four walls around you. Wood is best: with stone and metal, building a wall will take too much time. Moreover, aggressive players will not wait for your structure to accumulate its health points.

At the center of those four walls, build stairs. That will let you peep your head out to determine the enemy's position and, once he's in your line of fire, eliminate him.

In more dangerous situations, especially at the end of the match, build a three-story tower.

Follow the same principle: build four walls around you and stairs inside. This time, however, build another four walls on top of those you've already built. Then jump in order to put a second stairway under your feet. Now you have a two-story tower. You're not going to stop there, though: repeat those steps one more time.

Voilà: you've just created a three-story tower. It's entirely possible to build a tower that's even higher, but we don't recommend it: if a player shoots at the base of your tower and destroys it, the whole thing will collapse. A fall from higher than three stories will mean a heavy loss of health. So don't go higher than three stories, especially if you're high enough to target your enemies.

If those opponents give you the opportunity, always build a metal base.

That will pose a much greater challenge.

During the final minutes of the game, the fighting generally ends with explosive weapons. Plan for enough material to protect yourself and repair any damage.

The ideal solution at the end of the match would be to build an entirely metal tower, but without the resources and time, that's little more than a fantasy. You can, however, use stone, which is an excellent compromise.

Fortnite offers inventive and virtually limitless options for building. The three-story tower technique is the simplest to reproduce. But use your imagination and common sense. You also need to be able to get out of your structure at any time if danger approaches. Modify your structures, create doors, build new passageways by laying floors, construct another tower alongside the first one . . .

The idea is to give as little information as possible about your position and ensure you are protected but be able to return fire.

ROOFS

In *Fortnite Battle Royale*, players at a greater height have an advantage over their enemies. Your enemies will attempt to dominate you by every means possible and gain access to your structures from above. To prevent them from doing that, build a roof. You can even add a floor above your head (which in that case will serve as a ceiling). Your enemies will then need to destroy both the roof and the ceiling in order to enter. That will give you time to make your move and settle your score with them.

POSSIBLE MODIFICATIONS

Here are some ways you can modify structures to make them more useful during your matches. We recommend that you practice making them when you're out of harm's way. Then, when you feel ready, you can put that knowledge to work when faced with your enemies.

DOORS

CONSTRUCTION

WINDOWS

MEDIUM-SIZED WALLS

LOW WALLS

ARCHES

CONSTRUCTION

ARCHED CORNERS

SIMPLE CORNERS

SHELTERS

TENTS

CORNER STAIRWAYS

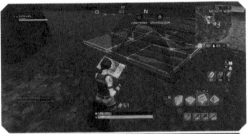

8. WINNING YOUR BATTLES

No two *Fortnite Battle Royale* matches are alike. *Fortnite* players are especially inventive and devise more and more strategies for eliminating their rivals. However, there are certainly some essential techniques for defending yourself, returning fire, and capturing the Holy Grail of being the top player!

ACCURATE AIM

Above all else, in order to win your battles, it's essential to know how to aim. If you're a beginner, you'll need to play a few games in order to learn the ropes.

You can shoot in several ways. The first is to shoot without pressing the aim button. That technique is not very accurate because the bullets are scattered widely. On the other hand, at short distances while you're in motion, that trick can pay off, especially with an assault rifle. When you hold down the aim button, the viewfinder shrinks. So your shots are much more accurate.

Lastly, there's a much better method for accurate shooting: don't move, crouch down, then aim at your enemy. Your viewfinder will appear even smaller than before, ensuring excellent shooting accuracy.

Remember! During the Battle Royale, when you're immobile, you're highly exposed to danger. So that technique is preferable when you're located fairly far from your enemy or you have shelter.

At a long distance, your preferred weapon will obviously be a sniper rifle. Its scope will ensure accuracy—if you know how to use it. If a player is located 300 meters from you, there's no point in aiming with the center of the viewfinder. You will have to evaluate the distance and adjust the viewfinder upward accordingly. When the bullet is shot from the gun barrel, it doesn't travel straight as an arrow; its height diminishes over a distance, and it's that decrease in height that you'll need to account for accurately. And as if that weren't enough, in most cases your enemies will be in constant motion. So it's no secret that you have to anticipate and plan for their actions and gestures. For example, if you see an enemy crossing a field from left to right, point your viewfinder to the right. The time to shoot is a second before the player passes in front of your viewfinder! With luck, your assailant will be hit.

If he hides behind a truck or a tree, prepare to shoot on the left. The *Fortnite* characters are right-handed, so your enemy will tend to move to the right of the obstacle—which is your left.

Remember not to stay motionless, and act in ways that can't be anticipated. Keep a cool head and don't try things that are impossible. Bear in mind that the goal in *Fortnite Battle Royale*, first and foremost, is survival.

SURVIVING A DUEL IN A BUILDING

In order to win a duel in a house, you will first have to guess where your enemy is located. Increase the volume on your headset and listen closely for the sound of footsteps. Then you'll be able to assess his or her location.

Always arm yourself with a shotgun in closed spaces. It's the weapon best suited to close combat. Avoid changing weapons every few seconds, because it's fairly noisy. You can also choose to wait for the other player to come in your direction. But that's a risky move.

A player who remains in one place is more vulnerable than a player in motion. It's better not to let your assailant take the initiative. So be proactive!

Crouch down in order to move more quietly. Use the furniture in the house and the angles of the walls to hide and gather information. Your character is right-handed, and that's important. When you're hiding behind a wall, try to keep your enemy on your right, and always move from left to right. That way you'll have a better view—and thus a better shooting angle—than you would if the enemy were on your left.

Use your traps and place them carefully in the house: above the entry door, above a stairway, next to a door, etc. Traps are extremely destructive because they eliminate 150 health.

Don't forget that players who are higher up have a better chance

 of eliminating their enemy. When you're above your opponents, you have their head in your firing line.

If your enemies are up above and you're down below, you'll

have better luck if you aim for their lower body . . . but they'll have the advantage.

If your enemy is inside a house and not moving, get some height, climb on the roof, and destroy it—but be careful not to

fall. Make sure you're not in the enemy's viewfinder at the moment the structure collapses. If possible, throw a few grenades, then finish him off!

WINNING A DUEL IN NATURE

If you're the first to spot your enemy, try a sniper shot, or else start with the assault rifle and continue shooting until you get your valuable kill.

If the enemy tries to build something for protection, you can continue shooting at those structures to make that impossible.

But be sure to check that you have enough ammunition for that. Consider putting up a wall in front of you to protect yourself, especially when you're forced to reload. That's a dangerous moment, when your victim may regain the upper hand.

If he's a fast builder, you can try to put pressure on him by building a "double stair/wall" to climb above him. Finish him off with a shotgun! Be careful not to make a headlong rush for it, because he may regain the advantage by destroying your stairs. In addition, try to build them from stone so that they're more robust.

Another approach is to move quietly and use items from your surroundings, rather than structures you build, to eliminate your enemy. The fact is that building gives information about your position.

Lastly, and still being quiet, you could decide to engage your enemy in combat by building a double metal stairway. Avoid wood and stone, because they make a lot more noise than metal. Once you're above your victim, blast him in the head with your shotgun.

If an enemy shoots at you first from above, immediately build four walls around you along with a stairway, so you can see where the shots are coming from and locate your assailant. If she's shooting nonstop, wait until she reloads before engaging in combat.

We advise you not to hide behind a tree for too long if at all possible. Players won't hesitate to destroy the tree in no time.

Exchanges of gunfire are noisy and could attract the attention of other players. Always stay on your guard.

CONFRONTING MULTIPLE ENEMIES

In solo mode, it's everyone for him or herself. If you see two players in combat not far off, let them fight to the death. When only one player remains, take advantage of his or her weakness and injuries and go on the attack. You'll kill that combatant easily. If you have a rocket launcher or grenade launcher, don't hesitate to use it to inflict major damage . . . and earn several kills at one blow.

At the end of the game, when the combat area is especially limited and filled with structures, stay attentive whenever you shoot at an enemy, because someone else may locate you by listening to your shots. Don't forget to build protection for yourself—that's essential. During the last few minutes of the game, walking on the ground amounts to suicide!

In duo or squad mode, use the same methods as in solo mode, and you'll have additional allies who can help you.

CONCLUSION

We hope this guide will be helpful in your quest for the top.

Remember that *Fortnite Battle Royale* is a game that combines strategy and creativity. Don't hesitate to try something new.

If you're a beginner, you won't become the best overnight; you'll need to practice in order to learn the variety of techniques. Don't get discouraged! Try every mode, every weapon! Never forget construction—it's as important as handling weapons.

But most of all, have fun!

And good luck in all the upcoming seasons!

Breaking news: while we were writing this, new locations, weapons, and other items were added to the game. We hope you'll be able to make the most of these! And sadly there are a few that have been retired and no longer exist in *Fortnite Battle Royale*.

ACKNOWLEDGMENTS

Writing this book has been a new experience for me, one that's extremely interesting and motivating.

My thanks go to 404 Éditions, and especially Lucie and Ludivine, who have helped me throughout this book's development.

A big thanks to Samantha Thiery, without whom I could never have completed this project.

And a special thanks to Tilah, whose valuable advice has proven essential.

Thanks to the entire *Fortnite* community and the YouTubers Gotaga, Wisethug, and Mickalow, who are helping to spread the game far and wide.

I'd also like to thank my girlfriend, Amandine, one of the most courageous people I've ever met. And thanks for supporting my evenings devoted to *Fortnite* without batting an eye!

Thanks to my fellow gamers: Maxime, Suji, Thomas, Damien, Dany, Charlton, Kevan, Adrian, and Okhan, all of whom are going to have to read this book!

Thanks to Will Shaw for your expert reading.

Lastly, I'd like to thank my mother, my grandparents, my uncle, and my family for their unfailing support during all my projects.

This book is dedicated to my Aunt Martine.